Sherlock Holmes and The Missing Portrait

Mabel Swift

Copyright © 2024 by Mabel Swift

www.mabelswift.com

All rights reserved.

No portion of this book may be reproduced in any form without written permission from the publisher or author. This is a work of fiction and any resemblance to anyone living or dead is purely coincidental.

Contents

Chapter One	1
Chapter Two	5
Chapter Three	11
Chapter Four	15
Chapter Five	19
Chapter Six	24
Chapter Seven	27
Chapter Eight	31
Chapter Nine	35
Chapter Ten	39
Chapter Eleven	42
Chapter Twelve	46
Chapter Thirteen	53
Chapter Fourteen	57

The Haunted Museum: A Sample	64
A note from the author	87

Chapter One

Inside the upper rooms of 221B Baker Street, Sherlock Holmes reclined in his well-worn armchair, the faint aroma of tobacco lingering in the air as he pored over the daily newspapers. Across from him, his steadfast companion, Dr John Watson, occupied his customary seat, his gaze alternating between the pages before him and the pensive expression upon his friend's countenance.

"It has been an eternity since our last case, Watson," Holmes remarked, his voice tinged with a hint of restlessness as he tossed aside the newspaper, its contents evidently failing to pique his insatiable curiosity. A wry smile played upon his lips, one eyebrow arched quizzically. "Has everyone taken a holiday away from London, perhaps? Or have people taken to solving their own mysteries?"

Watson chuckled. He set aside his newspaper with a contented sigh. "Patience, Holmes," he counselled, a glint of fond amusement dancing in his eyes as he regarded his restive companion. "Trouble has an uncanny knack for finding us, even in the most unlikely of circumstances."

As if on cue, the gentle knock upon the door preceded the entrance of their landlady, Mrs Hudson. Her kindly face crinkled into a warm smile as she made her way into the sitting room, proffering a sealed envelope.

"A message for you, Mr Holmes," she announced, clearly well-accustomed to acting as the intermediary for the various missives and enquiries that found their way to the celebrated detective.

Holmes straightened in his chair, eyes alight with renewed interest as he accepted the mysterious correspondence. Deftly breaking the seal with one long finger, he swiftly scanned the contents of the letter, his expression inscrutable.

"Well, Holmes?" Watson prompted. "What is the nature of this correspondence?"

"It would appear, my dear Watson, that we have been summoned by the Duchess of Rothbury," Holmes replied, his voice tinged with intrigue as he refolded the letter with deft movements. "The esteemed lady requests our assistance in a matter of delicate import and extends a gracious invitation to her stately residence in Mayfair. No doubt the nature of her predicament shall prove a stimulating diversion from the mundanities that have plagued us of late."

Watson's eyes widened in recognition at the mention of the illustrious name. "The Duchess of Rothbury? Why, I have heard many a tale of her lavish soirees and her tireless dedication to the social whirl of London's high society. Indeed, the Duchess has kept herself extremely occupied since the tragic passing of her beloved husband, the late Duke. Her philanthropic endeavours and patronage of the arts are renowned throughout the city's elite circles."

Holmes nodded sagely, his fingers steepled beneath his chin as he pondered the intriguing development. "A most curious summons, to be sure. This matter must be of a delicate nature indeed, to compel her to solicit our services. I must reply forthwith."

He reached for his pen and a fresh sheet of paper. "I shall inform the Duchess that we will pay her a visit this very afternoon."

With a flourish, Holmes inscribed his response, the nib of his pen scratching across the parchment with practised ease. He sealed the missive with a dab of crimson wax from the candle flickering nearby, imprinting it with the distinctive crest of his personal seal. Once the wax had cooled and hardened, securing the envelope's contents, he dashed downstairs in search of Mrs Hudson. He found her in the parlour, dusting the mantelpiece with her customary care and attention.

"Mrs Hudson, might I trouble you to arrange for the prompt delivery of this message?" he inquired, holding out the sealed envelope.

"Of course, Mr Holmes," she replied, taking the letter with a nod. Her eyes widened momentarily with undisguised interest as she glimpsed the name inscribed upon the envelope, but as discreet as always, she didn't voice her curiosity aloud and merely said, "I shall deal with this straight away."

She walked out of the parlour, leaving Holmes to his contemplations about the Duchess of Rothbury and why she needed their help.

Chapter Two

The hansom cab trundled to a halt before the grand façade of the Duchess of Rothbury's stately residence in Mayfair, the hooves of the horses clopping against the cobblestones as they came to a rest. Holmes stepped out first, casting an appraising eye over the imposing edifice before him. Dr Watson followed close behind, unable to entirely conceal his awe at the opulent surroundings.

"Impressive, is it not?" Holmes remarked, his voice laced with a hint of dry amusement as he took in his companion's reaction. "Though I dare say the true interest lies not in the outward trappings of wealth and status, but rather in the delicate mystery that awaits us within."

A liveried footman hastened to usher them into the resplendent foyer. The rich scents of polished wood and beeswax mingled with the faint, floral notes of abundant blooms in vases arranged around the area.

"This way, sirs," the footman intoned as he led them through the labyrinthine corridors towards the parlour, where the Duchess awaited their arrival.

As they entered the sumptuously appointed room, the Duchess rose from her seat, a gracious smile on her face as she extended her hand in welcome. "Mr Holmes, Dr Watson, how good of you to attend with such alacrity," she greeted them warmly. "I do hope the matter at hand proves a worthy diversion from your usual pursuits."

Holmes inclined his head respectfully, his keen gaze sweeping over the Duchess's form as he committed every nuance of her appearance and demeanour to his prodigious memory. "Your Grace," he replied smoothly, "you may rest assured that whatever matter concerns you shall receive the utmost dedication of my humble talents."

The Duchess gestured for them to be seated, her expression growing momentarily pensive as she collected her thoughts. "As I intimated in my missive, the nature of this affair is one of delicate import, requiring the utmost discretion. Early this morning, I received a delivery that has caused me no small degree of consternation."

She rose from her chair and crossed to a nearby side table, upon which rested a large, canvas-wrapped object.

She untied the cords securing the wrappings, allowing the fabric to fall away to reveal the portrait concealed beneath.

Watson's brows rose in surprise as he took in the image depicted upon the canvas. A striking portrayal of a man attired in a business suit, seated in what appeared to be a private library. "You see, gentlemen," the Duchess continued, "this is not, as I had anticipated, a portrait of my own likeness that I had commissioned from the esteemed artist, Julian Devaux. Instead, it depicts a gentleman entirely unknown to me, though I must confess his face does strike a faint chord of familiarity and I wonder if I've seen him at a social gathering recently. More unsettling, though, is the background, for this is my library, and it's the room I choose for my portrait. It's a mystery as to who this man is, and why he should be painted in my library."

Holmes' brow furrowed ever so slightly as he studied the canvas, his eyes narrowing in contemplation. "A most curious development, indeed," he murmured, his gaze flickering briefly towards the Duchess before returning to scrutinise the figure portrayed upon the canvas. "Might I enquire as to the specifics of your commission to Mr Devaux? Any pertinent details, no matter how seemingly insignificant, could prove invaluable in unravelling this perplexing conundrum."

The Duchess said, "Mr Devaux is widely renowned for his unparalleled talent in capturing the essence of his subjects through his exquisite portraiture. Opulent settings and aristocratic subjects have become synonymous with Devaux's name, and he has a long list of clients, some of whom are in my social circles. In the wake of my dear husband's passing, I felt compelled to commission a new portrait of myself in the library. It was a place where I spent many treasured hours with my husband."

Holmes and Dr Watson listened with an occasional nod of understanding.

The Duchess continued, and her eyes took on a distant look as she delved into the recollections. "Mr Devaux and I had several preliminary consultations, during which he would study me intently, committing every nuance of my features and bearing to his sketchpad. Once he had enough information, I chose my required gown and placed myself in the library. Mr Devaux spent many hours painting my portrait, but in line with his requirements, I was not permitted to see any part of the portrait until it was finished." She looked towards the portrait, her expression clearly conveying it was not at all what she'd been expecting.

Watson listened intently; his brow furrowed in concentration as he sought to piece together the puzzle before them. He said, "And yet, despite his meticulous preparations and your explicit commission, the portrait you received bears no semblance to you. A most baffling turn of events, to be sure."

The Duchess inclined her head, a troubled expression flickering across her refined features. "Precisely, Dr Watson," she affirmed. "As you can well imagine, I was quite taken aback upon unveiling this portrayal. Which makes me wonder if my likeness has been captured in another's house, perhaps seated in one of their rooms. As I said, Mr Devaux has a long list of clients, and I'm worried that the workload was too much for him and he made mistakes with his backgrounds and subjects. I sincerely hope someone isn't gazing upon my face instead of their own somewhere in London."

Holmes said sagely, "That's precisely what I am thinking, too."

The Duchess' voice dropped to a hushed tone as she confided her innermost concerns. "I fear the potential ramifications should word of this puzzling substitution become public knowledge. The notion of my true portrait being misplaced, or worse, misused in some untoward manner fills me with no small degree of trepidation. Not to mention, that I now have a portrait of a strange man in my library. What would people think?"

Holmes's eyes narrowed thoughtfully as he regarded the Duchess, his brilliant mind already whirring with potential theories and avenues of investigation. "Fear not, Your Grace," he assured her. "We shall endeavour to unravel this mystery. May I ask, how was the painting delivered to you?"

The Duchess replied, "It arrived at the tradesman's entrance a few hours ago and my butler placed it in here. Another puzzling element is the label that was attached to the outer wrapping. I still have it." She moved over to the sideboard and retrieved a piece of paper. She gave it to Holmes.

He read the words out loud, "'The Duchess of Rothbury's Library'. How peculiar. The painting is addressed to your library and not yourself. This only adds to the mystery. But I assure you, Your Grace, we will solve this puzzle for you."

The Duchess met his gaze levelly, a flicker of relief evident in her eyes. "Mr Holmes, Dr Watson, you have my sincere appreciation. My reputation, and the legacy of my late husband's noble name, rests in your most capable hands."

Chapter Three

With the Duchess' revelations still fresh in their minds, Sherlock Holmes and the good doctor wasted no time in securing the address of Mr Devaux's studio from her ladyship before biding her farewell.

"Come, Watson!" Holmes exclaimed, his long strides carrying him swiftly towards the waiting hansom cab. "The trail grows ever warmer, and we must pursue it with all haste lest it turn cold."

The artistic quarter of London, with its charming array of studios and galleries, proved to be their destination. The cab clattered to a halt before a nondescript edifice, its brick façade weathered by the elements yet exuding an undeniable air of creative energy.

Holmes rapped smartly upon the door of Mr Devaux, but their summons went unanswered. A frown creased his brow as he tried the handle, only to find it firmly secured against unwanted intrusion.

"Most peculiar," he murmured, his keen eyes scanning their surroundings for any clue or indication as to the artist's whereabouts.

It was at that moment that the sound of a door opening nearby caught their attention. A young man, his clothes liberally spattered with vibrant hues of paint, emerged from the neighbouring studio, his brow furrowed in mild annoyance at the disturbance.

"Can I be of assistance, gentlemen?" he inquired.

Holmes replied, "Indeed you can, sir. We are in search of Julian Devaux, the artist whose studio lies just here. Might you have any knowledge of his current whereabouts?"

The young man's expression shifted, a flicker of surprise crossing his features. "Devaux? Why, he departed most abruptly a few hours ago, bundling a few suitcases into a waiting carriage and making off with nary a word of explanation."

Watson's eyebrows rose in surprise at this revelation, and he exchanged a meaningful glance with his companion.

"Abruptly, you say?" Holmes pressed. "Most unlike an artist of such renown, I should think."

The man nodded. "Indeed. I was working intently on my art this morning, and the sudden commotion outside disturbed me. I looked out of my window and saw Devaux, hurrying out into the street with his belongings, hailing a cab with an almost frantic urgency. Most out of character, I must say, the man is usually a picture of composure and decorum."

Holmes' eyes narrowed thoughtfully. "I wonder what made him leave with such haste, and where he was going."

The young artist said, "He might turn up at his exhibition tonight. It's being held at a gallery on Bond Street. It's the unveiling of his latest works, or so I believe. If he's to make an appearance anywhere soon, it would surely be there. Would you like the gallery's name?"

Holmes said, "That would be most appreciated. Thank you."

The young man gave the details and said goodbye before hurrying back into his studio.

As Holmes and Watson retraced their steps towards the awaiting hansom cab, Holmes' expression was pensive, his mind already formulating a strategy for their next move.

"Well, Watson?" he remarked, "it would seem our elusive artist has taken flight, much like a startled bird fleeing its cage. But why? Has he realised what a commotion the delivery of his painting to the Duchess would yield? Was the painting a result of his overworked mind, as the Duchess suggested? We shall make our way to this art gallery this evening and see what truths might be revealed. If luck is on our side, we will meet the elusive Mr Devaux."

With a renewed sense of purpose, the pair climbed into the cab, already discussing why Julian Devaux had undertaken such a sudden departure, and if he would return that evening.

Chapter Four

As Sherlock Holmes and Dr Watson entered the art gallery later that evening, the low murmur of conversation drifted towards them, carrying with it an undercurrent of bewilderment and surprise. The assembled guests, all adorned in elegant attire, were engaged in hushed discussions around the framed artwork, their faces a mixture of confusion and intrigue.

"What was he thinking?" a woman remarked, her voice tinged with disapproval. "This isn't Devaux's usual style at all."

Mutters of agreement met her words.

Holmes' keen ears picked up on the comments. He strode forward, Watson close at his heels, eager to look upon the controversial works that had so captivated the gathered throng.

As they approached the first set of framed sketches, Holmes found himself momentarily taken aback by the stark black-and-white images that greeted him. He had been expecting sumptuous surroundings and noble-looking subjects. In their place were the everyday people of London's poorer districts, their faces etched with the signs of hard living and toil.

Yet, despite the grime and weariness that clung to their features, each subject wore a smile that seemed to radiate from within. More astonishing were the backgrounds that Devaux had sketched. They didn't convey the person's expected surroundings at all and were a mix of seemingly impossible environments.

"Extraordinary," Holmes said, his gaze roving over the assembled portraits. "Devaux has captured the people with an almost whimsical touch and he's placed them in entirely new environments. But why would he undertake such an enterprise?"

Dr Watson replied, "Perhaps his subjects asked him to. Maybe they wanted him to represent whatever dreams filled their sleeping hours."

Holmes nodded. "You could be right in that assumption. But let's continue looking and find evidence to support your theory."

Dr Watson pointed to the next framed image. "Why, Holmes, isn't that Sarah, the flower seller from Covent Garden?"

Indeed, there she was, the young woman's likeness rendered in exquisite detail. But instead of the bustling streets and market stalls that usually formed her backdrop, Sarah was depicted in a sprawling garden, surrounded by lush plants and towering trees. In her hands, she clutched a set of plans, the intricate designs hinting at landscape design.

Holmes smiled and said, "Having chatted with Sarah on a few occasions, I do recall that she often spoke about being a landscape designer. Yet, she always laughed as soon as she said those words as if it were an impossible dream. Perhaps she voiced those same words to Julian Devaux, hence the reason for creating this particular background. I wonder what Sarah thought of this image?"

"Maybe she never saw the finished sketch," Watson said. "But I'm sure it would be something that would bring a smile to her face."

As they moved further along the gallery wall, another familiar face caught their attention. Billy, the young chimney sweep who often delivered messages to their Baker Street lodgings, grinned up at them from the canvas, his soot-streaked face alight with joy.

But instead of the grime and detritus of his trade, Billy was on a stage and surrounded by the trappings of a magician's art—top hat, playing cards, and mysterious boxes hinting at illusions and magic.

"It appears the boy dreams of magic," Holmes mused. "I wouldn't put anything past Billy; he's a bright young man."

Watson chuckled softly, his heart warmed by the sight of Billy's infectious grin. "A noble aspiration, to be sure. And one that Devaux has captured with remarkable sensitivity."

As they continued their circuit of the gallery, Holmes and Watson found themselves confronted with portrait after portrait, each one a window into the hidden hopes and dreams of London's forgotten citizens. Seamstresses and factory workers, street urchins and labourers - all were represented, their faces suffused with a quiet dignity that belied their humble circumstances.

"One thing puzzles me," Watson said. "Why would Devaux choose to focus on these subjects, so far removed from his usual fare? And to have them display here for all to see?"

Holmes replied, "Questions that beg an answer, my dear Watson. And one that I suspect may lie at the very heart of our mystery."

Chapter Five

Holmes' eyes narrowed at the sound of the sneering voice that cut through the quiet murmurs of the gallery. He turned to find himself face-to-face with a man whose countenance seemed etched with bitterness and disdain.

"Mr Bartholomew Grange, I presume?" Holmes said coolly, recognizing the man who penned scathing critiques in many newspapers. It was said Bartholomew was a failed artist, and instead of taking up a new craft, he had taken the easier route of unleashing his frustrated anger upon others instead. His published words had earned him a certain notoriety in artistic circles.

Grange's lips curled into a contemptuous sneer as he raked his gaze over the assembled portraits. "So, you've deduced who I am, Mr Holmes. How utterly thrilling for you."

Watson bristled at the man's mocking tone, but Holmes raised a hand, forestalling any retort from his faithful companion.

"I take it you have some insight into Devaux's motivations for this particular exhibition?" he asked, his tone deceptively mild.

Grange snorted derisively. "Motivations? The man has clearly lost what little talent he possesses. For years, I told him that his work had grown stale, predictable. An endless parade of simpering aristocrats and vapid society beauties, all rendered with the same lifeless precision."

People turned around at his rising voice, giving him looks full of disgust.

That didn't stop Bartholomew Grange. His eyes glittered with a mixture of scorn and perverse delight as he gestured at the nearby sketches. "I dared him to produce something different, something that would actually stir the soul instead of lulling it to sleep. And this," he said, his voice thick with contempt, "is what he offers in response. Pathetic renderings of the unwashed masses, their vulgar grins mocking the very notion of art itself."

Holmes regarded the critic with a steady, appraising gaze. "I find your assessment somewhat lacking, Mr

Grange. To my eyes, Devaux has captured something far more profound than mere portraiture."

Grange opened his mouth to protest, but Holmes pressed on, undeterred.

"These sketches offer a glimpse into the lives and dreams of those often overlooked by polite society. The flower seller who longs to shape and cultivate gardens of beauty. The young chimney sweep whose spirit yearns for the magic and wonder of the stage." He gestured at the nearby images of Sarah and Billy, their faces alight with hope and aspiration. "Devaux has given voice to their dreams and captured them on canvas. Is that not the true purpose of art; to elevate the human spirit, to capture those fleeting moments that might otherwise be lost to the relentless march of time?"

Grange seemed momentarily taken aback by Holmes' impassioned defence, his mouth working soundlessly for a moment before he regained his composure.

"Pretty words, Mr Holmes," he sneered. "But who wants to gaze upon such commonplace subjects? Art should inspire, should elevate the viewer to loftier realms, not wallow in the squalor of the gutters."

A ghost of a smile played across Holmes' lips. "Ah, but therein lies the true genius of Devaux's work, my dear sir.

He has shown us that beauty and inspiration can be found in the most unexpected of places, if one only has the eyes to see it."

With that, Holmes turned away from the sputtering critic, his attention once more drawn to the portraits of Billy and Sarah. A thoughtful expression settled over his features as he studied the sketches, his mind already formulating a plan.

"Watson," he said, beckoning his friend closer. "I find myself quite taken with these particular works. I should like to purchase them, if the gallery owner is amenable."

Watson's brow furrowed in surprise. "But whatever for, Holmes?"

A warm smile spread across the detective's features, softening the usual sharp lines of his countenance. "Why, to gift them to young Billy and dear Sarah, of course. A small token, a reminder that their dreams and aspirations are worthy of being celebrated, no matter how lofty or fanciful they might seem."

As Holmes walked towards the gallery owner, Watson cast a fond smile at his friend. Despite Holmes' sometimes cold and calculating demeanour, there lay a warm-heartedness that often surprised him.

And as they departed the gallery, the carefully wrapped sketches tucked under Holmes' arm, Watson asked in which direction their investigation should take next. All he received from Holmes in reply was an enigmatic smile.

Chapter Six

Upon arriving at Covent Garden the next morning, Holmes scanned the bustling throngs with a keen eye until he espied the familiar figure of Sarah, the flower seller. Her bright smile lit up her face as she hawked her wares to the passing crowds.

"Good day to you, Miss Sarah," Holmes called out, drawing her attention.

"Why, Mr Holmes! And Dr Watson too," she replied, bobbing a little curtsy. "Whatever brings you here this morning? Would you like some flowers? I have plenty to choose from."

Holmes declared, "We shall acquire some blooms during our visit, but our purpose here is of a more delightful nature." He extracted one of the framed portraits tucked securely under his arm and offered it to her. "I believe this rightly belongs in your possession. Mr Devaux exhibited it in a gallery the previous evening, and I could not resist purchasing it for you."

Sarah gasped, her eyes growing wide as she took in the exquisite image of herself amidst a lush garden, plans clutched in her hands. "Oh, Mr Devaux...he did capture my dream so beautifully, didn't he?" She blushed, averting her eyes shyly. "When he asked if he might sketch me a few weeks ago, I'll confess I was flattered, but thought little of it at the time. But as he worked, he asked about my life and my hopes for the future. I found myself admitting how I longed to design landscapes one day. I had no idea he was going to put this background in his sketch. He did ask if I'd give him permission to display the sketch in public. I said yes, but I thought he was jesting, because who would want to see me?"

Holmes gave her a slight bow. "Many people would, and many people did last night. In my opinion, it is one of the most exquisite pieces of art that I have ever set my eyes upon, and it's down to Mr Devaux's talent and the sparkle in your eyes, Miss Sarah."

Sarah smiled. "Thank you, Mr Holmes." She looked at the image and sighed wistfully. "If only this picture was real. If only this was how my life could be."

Watson smiled warmly at the young woman. "And why can't it be? All great works start with a dream, Miss Sarah."

"Quite so," Holmes agreed with a nod. "I do hope this portrait shall serve as inspiration to pursue your dreams. The world is in sore need of more beauty."

Her blush deepened, but her eyes shone with renewed determination. "You're right, Mr Holmes. Seeing this picture makes it seem more real somehow. I'll do what it takes to make it happen. I don't know what or how! But I'll make a start. Thank you so kindly for buying this for me, Mr Holmes."

With a smile, the detective dismissed her gratitude, remarking, "The pleasure is mine. Now then, which floral arrangements shall we buy from your offerings today?"

Upon concluding their acquisitions, Holmes and Dr Watson bid Sarah farewell and commenced their quest to locate Billy, the youthful chimney sweeper. Regrettably, he proved elusive, but after inquiring about his whereabouts from his companions, they were assured Billy would be told of their inquiries and would seek them out in due course.

Chapter Seven

Later that morning, Holmes rapped the brass knocker against the Duchess of Rothbury's front door with a decisive hand. Whilst awaiting a response, he turned to his companion. "What do you make of those sketches I bought from the gallery last evening, Watson?"

"Quite remarkable, Holmes," replied Watson, admiring the bouquet of flowers in his hand that they had purchased from young Sarah earlier. "Devaux has an extraordinary talent for capturing the human spirit, does he not?"

Before Holmes could respond, the door swung open, revealing the Duchess' maid. "Good day, sirs. I'm afraid her Grace is not at home at present."

"I see. We have arrived unannounced, and please, forgive us for disturbing you," Holmes said with an apologetic smile. "Could we leave a message with you? Please inform the Duchess that Sherlock Holmes and Dr Watson called to provide an update on the matter she hired us to investigate. Additionally, we would be most obliged if we could take another look at the painting that the Duchess received yesterday. If you have the time, of course."

The maid's eyes widened slightly at the request, but she nodded. "Very well, Mr Holmes. If you'll follow me."

They were led into the Duchess' parlour, where the mysterious portrait was leaning against the wall. Holmes wasted no time in crossing the room and examining it intently through his lens.

"Anything of interest?" Watson inquired, joining his companion.

"Indeed, Watson." Holmes' eyes narrowed as he focused his keen gaze on a small detail upon the subject's lapel. "Do you see that insignia there? A badge of some sort, it would seem?"

Watson leaned in closer, squinting slightly as he attempted to discern the minute detail his friend had noticed. "Why, yes, I do believe you're right, Holmes. A curious emblem of sorts adorns the lapel."

"I recognize that emblem," Holmes declared. "It belongs to the elite Lionsgate Club, one of London's most prestigious and exclusive gentlemen's establishments. Membership is strictly by invitation only, but I may be able to secure our admittance if needs be. We should go there immediately and search out this gentleman."

Prior to their departure from the residence, Dr Watson expressed his gratitude to the maid and presented her with the floral arrangement, asking if she could give it to the Duchess. She dipped into a respectful curtsy and affirmed that she would carry out the request.

She hesitated before turning away, and Holmes sensed she wished to tell them something.

He smiled kindly and asked, "Is there something you wish to say to us?"

"Yes, Mr Holmes," she replied hesitantly. "I hope I'm not speaking out of turn, but the Duchess showed me that unusual portrait, and I recognised the man because I used to work for him a few years ago. I told the Duchess his name, and she said she would let you know his identity when you next called on her. Would you like to know the man's name now? Or should that be something that the Duchess tells you?"

Holmes broke into a wide smile. "My dear girl, it would save us a lot of time and trouble if you could give us his name now. I'm sure the Duchess would appreciate your assistance with our investigation."

The maid gave him a smile of relief. "Thank you, Mr Holmes. His name is Sir Reginald Baxter, and he's usually at his club at this time of the morning."

Holmes and Watson thanked the maid for her invaluable help. They took their leave and hailed a hansom cab to transport them across London to the club's grand headquarters.

Chapter Eight

Holmes and Watson arrived at the grand entrance of the Lionsgate Club, an imposing structure that exuded an air of exclusivity and refinement. With a confident stride, Holmes approached the doorman, who regarded them with a scrutinizing gaze.

"Good afternoon, gentlemen," the doorman said, his voice polite yet firm. "May I inquire as to your business here?"

Holmes produced a calling card from his pocket and handed it to the doorman. "Sherlock Holmes and Dr John Watson. We are here to see Sir Reginald Baxter on a matter of some urgency."

The doorman examined the card, his eyebrows raising slightly in recognition. "Ah, Mr Holmes. Please wait here while I inform Sir Reginald of your arrival."

As they waited in the foyer, Watson marvelled at the grandeur of the surroundings. "I say, Holmes, this is quite an impressive establishment. How did you manage to secure our admittance?"

Holmes smiled enigmatically. "Let us just say that I have cultivated certain connections over the years, Watson. Ah, here comes Sir Reginald now. I recognise him from the painting."

A distinguished-looking gentleman approached them, his face a mixture of curiosity and puzzlement. "Mr Holmes, Dr Watson, you wanted to see me?"

Holmes wasted no time in explaining their purpose. "Sir Reginald, we are here on behalf of the Duchess of Rothbury. She recently received a painting from the artist Julian Devaux, depicting a man who bears a striking resemblance to yourself, seated in her library. She was most astonished as she was expecting a portrait of herself."

Sir Reginald's eyes widened in surprise. "How extraordinary! I must confess, I am both puzzled and intrigued by this revelation. As it happens, I also commissioned a painting from Devaux, and only yesterday, I received that portrait, but it was not at all what I expected."

Holmes leaned forward. "Pray tell, Sir Reginald, what did this portrait depict?"

"A young woman, seated in my office chair, wearing a striking red dress. I have never seen her before in my life. I had a lot of explaining to do to my dear wife, I can tell you! There was something strange thing about the label that came with the delivery. It was addressed to, 'Sir Reginald Baxter's Office', which I considered to be rather formal and not in keeping with Devaux's friendly manner."

Holmes exchanged a glance with Watson. "Sir Reginald, might we impose upon you to view this portrait? I believe it may shed some light on the mystery at hand."

Sir Reginald readily agreed. "Of course, gentlemen. My residence is nearby. Please, accompany me, and I shall show you the painting."

A short while later, they arrived at Sir Reginald's impressive home. As they entered the study, Holmes's glance immediately went to the portrait in question. A flicker of recognition crossed his face as he examined the image of the young woman in the red dress.

"Why, that is Miss Clara Simmons, a rising star in London's theatre scene," Holmes declared. "Dr Watson and I had the pleasure of attending one of her performances recently. She is quite talented."

Sir Reginald looked at Holmes in astonishment. "You know this woman, Mr Holmes?"

Holmes nodded. "Indeed, I do. And I believe I may have an inkling as to why Devaux chose to depict her in your portrait."

Holmes proceeded to recount their discoveries about the sketches Devaux had made of other people, and how he'd captured their dream lives. Sir Reginald listened intently, a smile gradually spreading across his face.

"How fascinating," he mused. "I must admit, I had often spoken to Devaux about my desire for a simpler life, one where I could sit in a library with nothing to do but read books. It seems he has taken those conversations to heart and incorporated them into his art, albeit in a painting that was meant for the Duchess of Rothbury. I would quite like to see that portrait, even purchase it if that's possible. I will send the Duchess a message and request a visit."

As they took their leave, Holmes and Watson felt they were one step closer to unravelling the mystery behind the Duchess's painting and the enigmatic artist behind it.

Chapter Nine

Holmes and Watson made their way to the theatre where Miss Clara Simmons was currently rehearsing. Upon their arrival, they were greeted by the bustling activity of the stage crew and the distant echoes of performers practising their lines.

After a brief conversation with the stage manager, they were directed to Miss Simmons' dressing room. Holmes rapped gently on the door, and a melodious voice called out, "Come in!"

As they entered, Miss Simmons looked up from her script. "Mr Holmes, Dr Watson! To what do I owe the pleasure of your visit?"

Holmes smiled politely and began to explain the purpose of their visit. "Miss Simmons, we are here on a rather peculiar matter involving the artist Julian Devaux and a series of paintings he has recently completed."

Miss Simmons gave them a confused look. "Devaux? Why, I recently received a painting from him. What a coincidence. But what does that have to do with you, Mr Holmes?"

Watson stepped forward, his voice gentle. "It appears that Devaux has been creating portraits that depict his subjects in rather unexpected settings, often reflecting their innermost desires or aspirations."

Holmes nodded in agreement. "Indeed, and it seems that you, Miss Simmons, have been featured in a painting commissioned by Sir Reginald Baxter, depicting you seated in his office chair."

Clara's eyes widened in surprise, and a bemused smile played upon her lips. "Me? In Sir Reginald's office? How extraordinary! I must admit, I've always dreamed of being a businesswoman and having my own office one day. It was something I discussed with Devaux during our sittings."

Holmes's eyes sparkled with intrigue. "I thought that might be the case, as you have often mentioned that particular aspiration to me. The painting that was delivered to you, Miss Simmons, might we see it?"

Clara nodded eagerly and led them to a corner of her dressing room where a large canvas was propped up against the wall. As Holmes and Watson examined the painting, they saw a woman who was clearly not Clara, relaxing in a dressing room similar to the one they were currently standing in.

"Why, that's Lady Lavinia Ashford!" Watson exclaimed. "The renowned botanist! She works at Kew Gardens."

Clara laughed. "Indeed, it is! I was quite surprised when I first saw it as I was expecting to see myself in the painting. But now, hearing about my appearance in Sir Reginald's painting, it all makes sense. He's been placing his subjects in the life they dream of, rather than the life they are living. And isn't it strange how someone else's normal life can be the subject of another person's dream?"

Holmes smiled. "How astute of you. Miss Simmons, did Devaux share much about himself during your sittings?"

Clara shook her head. "No, he was quite the listener, but he rarely spoke about himself. He seemed more interested in understanding his subjects and their innermost thoughts."

Watson smiled warmly. "It seems Devaux has a gift for not only capturing the likeness of his subjects but the rare gift of really listening to a person."

Clara nodded in agreement. "Indeed, he does. I would love to have that painting of myself in Sir Reginald's office.

It could inspire me to think seriously about my ambitions. I shall contact him and see if he will sell it to me."

Holmes clasped his hands together. "A splendid idea, Miss Simmons. Having met him recently, I am sure he will readily agree. One more question, if I may? Do you still have the label for the painting?"

Clara shook her head. "Sorry, I don't. I've already disposed of it. The wording was ever so peculiar. What was it now? Oh, yes. The words were, 'Miss Simmons' Dressing Room'. But now that you've told me what's happened, it makes sense. I think!"

Holmes smiled as if it was precisely the information he was expecting.

As Holmes and Watson took their leave, they thanked Miss Simmons for her time and assistance, their minds already racing with the possibilities of what they might discover when they met with Lady Lavinia Ashford.

Chapter Ten

Holmes and Watson stepped out into the crisp London air, their minds awhirl with the revelations gleaned from their conversation with Miss Simmons. As they navigated the bustling streets, dodging carriages and passers-by, Watson gave voice to the doubts plaguing his thoughts.

"I must confess, Holmes, I harbour a growing unease that we may be embarking on a wild goose chase," he remarked. "If Devaux has delivered a multitude of new paintings in recent weeks, we could find ourselves lost in an extensive search for the Duchess's elusive portrait. The prospect of spending countless days, or even weeks, tracking down each and every one of his commissions is a daunting one indeed!"

Holmes replied, "Worry not, my dear Watson. We shall follow one clue at a time, and the truth will reveal itself in due course. Our task may seem daunting, but with perseverance and a keen eye for detail, I have no doubt that we shall locate the Duchess's missing portrait."

Their next stop was the resplendent Kew Gardens, where they sought out the esteemed Lady Lavinia Ashford. The renowned botanist, known for her extensive knowledge of exotic flora, was overseeing the installation of a new and highly anticipated exhibition when the intrepid duo approached her. After explaining the peculiar situation surrounding the proliferation of Devaux's portraits and the curious case of the Duchess's missing likeness, Lady Ashford smiled knowingly, her eyes gleaming with a hint of intrigue.

"Ah, yes, I too had the pleasure of commissioning Mr Devaux to paint my portrait," Lady Ashford revealed, her eyes twinkling with fond memories. "During our sittings, we engaged in the most delightful conversations about my secret dreams and aspirations. I've always harboured a deep-seated desire to take to the stage, perhaps not as a full-time pursuit, but rather as an occasional indulgence. It was a whimsical fancy I felt compelled to share with him, knowing that he would understand the yearning of an artist's soul."

Holmes, his curiosity thoroughly aroused by Lady Ashford's revelation, leaned forward slightly. "Lady Ashford," he began, his voice low and conspiratorial, "have you, perchance, been the recipient of an unusual portrait yourself? One that might shed light on the mystery at hand?"

The accomplished botanist's eyes sparkled with barely contained mischief, her lips curving into an enigmatic smile. "Indeed, I have, Mr Holmes," she confirmed. "However, I believe it would be most prudent if you and your esteemed colleague, Dr Watson, were to pay a visit to my home later on today, perhaps around six this evening? I'm afraid I cannot, in good conscience, divulge the intriguing details of the painting in such a public setting, lest we attract unwanted attention."

Watson, his curiosity growing by the second, exchanged a meaningful glance with Holmes, silently communicating his intrigue. He said, "Of course, Lady Ashford. We shall most certainly call upon you later, at the appointed hour."

Chapter Eleven

Sherlock Holmes and Dr John Watson arrived at the stately home of Lady Ashford later that evening. Holmes reached out a slender finger and pressed the bell, which echoed with a sonorous chime inside the grand house. After a brief moment, the large oak door swung open, revealing a stern-faced butler who greeted them with a curt nod and ushered the detective and his companion inside.

As Holmes and Watson followed the butler into the drawing room, a sense of anticipation hung in the air. The room was dimly lit, with the flickering glow of the fireplace casting dancing shadows on the walls. In the centre of the room stood an easel, upon which a portrait was covered by a simple white sheet.

Lady Ashford smiled at Holmes and Watson. "Gentlemen," she began. "Thank you for coming to see me. I must confess that I know the identity of the person in this portrait. However, I hesitated to contact her, considering the nature of the image."

Holmes raised an eyebrow. "Please, do go on, Lady Ashford. We are most intrigued."

Lady Ashford continued, "You see, the sketches for this portrait were done in the small garden of my country cottage about a month ago. It's a rather secluded spot, and I'm afraid I took the liberty of wearing trousers, which, as a lady, I'm not supposed to do. But I often do things that are not expected of me, and quite honestly, I seldom give a hoot about other's opinions. But I must admit, trousers are terribly comfortable and I couldn't resist wearing them for my painting. As the portrait was intended to be hung only in the bedroom of my country home, I instructed Mr Devaux to sketch me in my leisurely attire—the trousers and a comfy shirt."

With a flourish, she removed the sheet, revealing the portrait beneath. Holmes and Watson took in every detail. The painting depicted the Duchess of Rothbury standing beside an apple tree in a charming garden, clad in trousers and a comfortable shirt. The Duchess's expression was one of relaxation and contentment, a stark contrast to her usual societal persona.

"The Duchess of Rothbury!" Watson exclaimed. "I must say, I never imagined her in such garments."

Holmes, however, remained focused on the portrait, his keen eyes studying every brushstroke. "Lady Ashford," he said, turning to face their host, "am I correct in assuming that you and the Duchess are close friends?"

Lady Ashford nodded. "Yes, Mr Holmes, we are. And I fear that she will be quite shocked to see herself portrayed in such a manner. It is not something she would typically allow."

Holmes stepped closer to the portrait, his mind already working through the implications. "Lady Ashford, with your permission, I would like to take this painting with me. I assure you, I will use the utmost tact when explaining the situation to the Duchess."

Lady Ashford hesitated for a moment, then nodded her assent. "Of course, Mr Holmes. I trust your judgment in this matter. Please, do what you think is best."

As Holmes carefully removed the portrait from the easel, Dr Watson turned to Lady Ashford, a question forming on his lips. "Lady Ashford, if I may ask, why did you choose to have your portrait painted in such an unconventional manner and not in a more formal setting such as your lovely home here?"

The lady smiled, a wistful look in her eyes. "Dr Watson, sometimes we all yearn for a bit of freedom from the constraints of society. The garden at my country cottage is my sanctuary, a place where I can be myself without fear of judgement. When Mr Devaux asked to paint my portrait, I saw it as an opportunity to capture a moment of true happiness and comfort. I wonder if he actually did complete that image of me in my garden. I would love to see it. Mr Holmes, would that be something you could look into for me?"

Holmes, having secured the portrait, turned to face Lady Ashford once more. "Of course. If such a painting exists, I will ensure it is delivered to you."

With that, Sherlock Holmes and Dr Watson bid their farewells to Lady Ashford and stepped out into the cool night air, the portrait of the Duchess of Rothbury safely in their possession. As they made their way back to Baker Street, Holmes' mind was already racing, piecing together the clues and forming a plan to unravel the mystery of the misplaced portraits to their client.

Chapter Twelve

Early the next morning, just as the sun was beginning to peek through the curtains of 221B Baker Street, Holmes sent an urgent message to the Duchess of Rothbury to see if they could call upon her as soon as possible as they had some important information to impart to her. Whilst waiting for her reply, Holmes and Watson enjoyed a breakfast together, sipping their tea and musing over what the Duchess's reaction would be when she laid eyes upon the painting of herself clad in such unusual, and possibly shocking, attire.

A reply arrived within two hours from the Duchess, inviting Holmes and Watson to visit her that very afternoon at her Mayfair residence.

A few hours later, Holmes gathered the painting, safely shrouded by the white sheet, and the two companions set off for the Duchess's home, eager to share their discovery with her.

Upon their arrival, the Duchess greeted them warmly; her smile was genuine though a hint of anxiety played across her fine features as she glanced at the wrapped object in Holmes' possession. She ushered them into her lavish drawing room, offering them a seat and a cup of tea.

"Mr Holmes, Dr Watson, thank you ever so much for coming. I trust you have some news regarding my missing portrait?"

Holmes nodded as he regarded the Duchess with concern. "Indeed, your Grace. We have successfully located your portrait, but I must warn you, it is not the one you are expecting. I'm afraid the circumstances surrounding its appearance and subsequent recovery are rather unusual, to say the least." He placed the covered portrait against the wall.

The Duchess frowned. "Unusual? In what way, Mr Holmes?"

Holmes said, "I have reached the conclusion that during your sittings with Mr Devaux, you may have discussed your dreams of a simpler life, away from the constraints and expectations of society. Am I correct in my assumptions?"

The Duchess averted her gaze. "Well, yes, I suppose I did," she admitted. "One does tend to chat during those long hours of posing, to pass the time and ease the tedium. But what has that to do with my missing portrait, Mr Holmes?"

Watson cleared his throat. "Your Grace," he began, "it appears that Mr Devaux took those intimate conversations to heart and decided to paint you not as you are, but as you might wish to be."

The Duchess looked from one man to the other. "I don't understand. Please, do explain more."

With a flourish, Holmes removed the sheet, revealing the Duchess in her casual attire, standing amidst the picturesque garden. The vibrant colours of the blooming flowers and the lush greenery seemed to come to life on the canvas, creating a stunning backdrop for the Duchess's unconventional portrait.

The Duchess gasped, her delicate hand flying to her mouth. "Oh, my word!" she exclaimed, her voice trembling. "Is that me? Am I truly wearing trousers in that portrait?"

Holmes nodded sagely, his keen eyes observing the Duchess's reaction. "It appears that Mr Devaux desired to immortalise you in a moment of genuine happiness, one he imagined as a result of your conversations with him."

The Duchess continued to stare at the painting, her expression a complex mix of emotions that seemed to shift and change with each passing second. "I see. But the potential repercussions if this portrait were to be seen by the wrong eyes! The scandal it could ignite would be catastrophic."

Watson's voice was reassuring as he said, "Your Grace, if I may be so bold, the painting was discovered in the safekeeping of your dear friend, Lady Ashford. She had no intention of revealing it to anyone else, and we can assure you that its existence will remain a closely guarded secret."

The Duchess nodded slowly. "That was most kind of her." Her attention was still fixed on the painting. A slow smile began to form on her face. "Mr Devaux painted me as I truly yearned to be, didn't he? Not the Duchess, not the stately society matron, but simply me. The real woman beneath it all. A woman who would love to relax and unwind in a beautiful garden in wonderful solitude."

Holmes nodded slowly, his own gaze studying the painting with a keen appreciation. "It appears so, your Grace. It is a rather striking likeness indeed. Mr Devaux has captured your essence most exquisitely."

A wistful expression spread across the Duchess' elegant features. "I look happy in that painting. Truly, genuinely happy. As if a great weight has been lifted from my soul and I am finally free to be myself once more. I haven't seen myself looking like that in years."

A hush descended upon them as they contemplated the intricacies of the portrait.

The Duchess of Rothbury turned to face Holmes and Watson, her eyes glistening with the sheen of unshed tears. "I cannot begin to express my gratitude, Mr Holmes, Dr Watson. Not merely for your diligence in locating this portrait, but for opening my eyes to the realisation that perhaps it is not such a terrible thing to dream of a different life, even if that life only exists within the brushstrokes of a painting."

Holmes bowed his head respectfully. "It was our distinct pleasure to be of service, your Grace. And if I may offer you a small piece of wisdom? Hold fast to that dream, nurture it deep within your heart. For it is the capacity to dream, to imagine a better world, that makes us fundamentally human, after all."

The Duchess smiled softly. "I shall most definitely take that to heart. Moreover, this portrait has sown the seeds of change within my very soul. Perchance the time has arrived for me to embrace a simpler existence, in some tranquil rural haven. I am moved to embark upon this path forthwith. To seize the day while my courage is strong, as it were." A soft laugh escaped her. "Perhaps I shall even request that my seamstress fashion me a pair of trousers. They have the appearance of being exceedingly comfortable."

Her statement brought forth warm smiles from Holmes and Watson.

The Duchess asked, "I must thank Mr Devaux immediately. Have you managed to speak to him? Did you catch him at his studio?"

"Alas, he has made a sudden departure from his place of work," Holmes advised. "But we shall track him down and find out why he decided to create this painting."

The Duchess nodded. "When you do find him, please express my sincere gratitude to him for painting this wonderful image of me."

Holmes assured her they would. He added, "If Mr Devaux completed your original commission, would you like us to arrange the delivery of it?"

The Duchess looked back at the painting leaning against the wall. "I would like that, Mr Holmes. Yet, in all honesty, I prefer the one you have brought to me today. I may even find the courage to display it in my hallway, just to see the look on my guests' faces! My goodness, what sort of a woman am I turning into?" Her smile was carefree and lit up her face.

Holmes and Watson smiled at the Duchess, who looked much happier than when they had first met her.

As they departed the residence and strolled down the street, Watson enquired, "If Mr Devaux captured you within a canvas, how would you be occupying yourself? What vision would your ideal existence resemble?"

A wistful expression passed fleetingly over Holmes's angular features. "My dear Watson," he began, his rich baritone voice warm with fondness, "I am already living it. A challenging career that engages my mind and tests my abilities. A faithful companion who stands steadfastly by my side through every twist and turn. And the endless mysteries of London waiting at my very doorstep, each one a new puzzle to unravel. In truth, what more could a man possibly ask for? Now, let's continue with our investigation as all the loose ends have not yet been tied up."

Chapter Thirteen

As Holmes and Watson strolled briskly along the street, a young soot-faced boy came running up to them, his worn shoes slapping against the stones.

"Mr Holmes! Dr Watson!" the lad called out excitedly as he caught up with the two gentlemen, a big grin spreading across his grimy face. "My pals down the way, said you were looking for me. Do you need my help with one of those grand investigations of yours? I'm always keen to lend a hand, I am!"

Holmes smiled warmly at the eager young lad. "Billy, my boy, you're just the person we were hoping to see. Indeed, we have a gift for you, a token of appreciation for your invaluable assistance in our investigations. But first, let us retire to the comfort of our humble abode on Baker Street, where we can discuss matters further."

Billy's eyes widened with a mix of excitement and trepidation. "But Mr Holmes, sir, I'm not fit to be seen in a fine house like yours. I'm covered in soot from head to toe, I am!"

Holmes chuckled. "Nonsense, Billy. A little soot never hurt anyone. In fact, I daresay it adds to your charm. Now, come along, and we'll explain everything in no time."

The trio made their way to 221B Baker Street, with Billy chattering excitedly about the possibilities of his mysterious gift.

Upon entering the house, Holmes called out to their landlady. "Mrs Hudson, would you be so kind as to provide young Billy here with a sheet to sit upon? We wouldn't want to soil your lovely sofa."

Mrs Hudson appeared, a warm smile gracing her features. "Of course, Mr Holmes. I'll fetch one right away. And perhaps a spot of tea and biscuits for our young guest?"

"Capital idea, Mrs Hudson," Holmes replied, as Billy grinned from ear to ear.

Once Billy was settled on the sofa, a sheet beneath him and a cup of tea on the table in front, Holmes retrieved the sketch from his desk. "Billy, my lad, Dr Watson and I came across this at an exhibition featuring the works of one Julian Devaux. We thought you might like to have it."

He handed the sketch to Billy, whose eyes grew wide with wonder as he took in the image of himself, surrounded by the tools of a magician. "Blimey, Mr Holmes! That's me, that is! But I'm dressed like a proper magician, with all them fancy props and whatnot. How did this happen?"

Holmes smiled knowingly. "It seems, Billy, that Mr Devaux has a keen eye for the aspirations of others. He asked about your dreams, did he not?"

Billy nodded, still transfixed by the sketch. "He did, sir. We often chatted when I met him on the streets. I told him how I'd love to be a magician, performing on stage and making people smile. But I never thought he'd go and draw me like this!"

"Well, Billy," Holmes said, "perhaps this is a sign that you should pursue your dream. I'll put in a good word for you at the local theatre. Every great magician needs to start somewhere, and an assistant's role could be just the ticket."

Billy's face lit up with joy. "You'd do that for me, Mr Holmes? Oh, thank you, sir! Thank you!"

Dr Watson, who had been observing the exchange with a fond smile, spoke up. "Billy, did Mr Devaux happen to mention anything about his own dreams or aspirations?"

Billy thought for a moment, then nodded. "He did, Dr Watson. He spoke of a cottage in Cornwall, where he hoped to retire someday. Said he'd paint pictures of the sea, just for his own pleasure. But he reckoned he might never get there, being so busy with work and all."

Holmes and Watson exchanged a meaningful glance. "Cornwall, you say?" Holmes mused. "Did he mention a specific location, by any chance?"

Billy shook his head. "No, sir. Just that it was in Cornwall and he looked right happy when he talked about it. I hope he gets to go there someday."

Holmes leaned back in his chair, steepling his fingers beneath his chin. "A cottage in Cornwall, a dream of painting the sea. Intriguing. It seems our Mr Devaux is a man of many layers, Watson."

Watson nodded in agreement. "Indeed, Holmes. And perhaps this information could help us solve the final parts of this mystery."

Chapter Fourteen

Billy lingered a while longer with Holmes and Watson, eagerly discussing his aspirations of becoming a magician and how he planned to make that dream a reality. With a twinkle in his eye, he vowed that once he had achieved fame and success, he would always ensure that they had complimentary tickets to his performances. His infectious enthusiasm soon had Holmes and Watson chuckling along with him, caught up in his excitement.

Before long, however, it was time for Billy to take his leave. Mrs Hudson, ever the thoughtful hostess, kindly provided Billy with a sheet to carefully wrap up the painting for safe transport. She also pressed a wrapped packet of biscuits into his hands, insisting that she had baked far too many and that Billy would be doing her a great favour by taking them off her hands. Billy expressed his gratitude, his eyes shining with pure delight at her generosity.

A few minutes later, as Holmes and Watson settled into their chairs, a nervous-looking man was shown into the room by Mrs Hudson. He introduced himself as Albert, Julian Devaux's long-time assistant, and explained that he had heard they were looking for Mr Devaux and he assumed it was due to the recent delivery of some unusual paintings. With an agitated air and a slight tremble in his voice, he confessed that the unfortunate mix-up of the portraits was entirely his doing, and he was deeply remorseful for the trouble it had caused.

"You see, Mr Holmes," Albert began, wringing his hands anxiously, "Mr Bartholomew Grange's relentlessly harsh words and scathing critiques had finally gotten to Mr Devaux. In a rare moment of daring, he decided to paint two portraits for each of his paying clients—the expected formal one and a second, more intimate piece capturing their secret dream life. He intended to keep the latter hidden away in his studio, hoping to one day discreetly approach his clients and offer them the additional portrait as a surprise gift."

Holmes kept his keen eyes fixed on Albert. "And what happened then, Albert?"

"I'm afraid I delivered the wrong portraits, Mr Holmes," Albert admitted, his voice trembling with remorse. "In my haste to distribute the paintings, I didn't read the labels properly and I mixed up the formal portraits with the intimate ones, delivering the wrong ones to the unsuspecting clients. When Mr Devaux realised the dreadful mistake, he was overcome with panic and decided to leave London. He said that everyone would blame him for the embarrassing mix-ups and not me. He sent me a telegram a few hours ago from a cottage in Cornwall, saying he has decided to stay there indefinitely and enjoy a simpler life, far away from the chaos and potential scandal he left behind in the city."

Albert looked so utterly distraught that Holmes felt compelled to offer some words of comfort. He said, "Albert, it seems your mistake may have inadvertently led to a positive change in the lives of the people who commissioned those paintings. So, in hindsight, your mistake has turned into an interesting form of fate, guiding them towards the lives they always yearned for but never dared pursue."

The relief was visible upon Albert's face. "Really? You think everything has turned out for the best?"

Holmes nodded. "I do. Albert. How many unusual paintings did Mr Devaux create?"

Albert replied, "There were four. He was going to do more but, well, because of my error, he's left London."

Holmes said, "You'll be relieved to know that we have seen all four of those paintings and spoken to the recipients. Everything is in order, and really, you have no need to be concerned. May I ask, do you still have the keys to Mr Devaux's studio?"

"I do," Albert replied.

"Would you be kind enough to deliver the portraits that were commissioned by Mr Devaux's clients? The expected ones, that is, for now. I know Lady Ashford is keen to receive hers."

"Of course, Mr Holmes. I'll go to the studio straight away. Is there anything else I can do? I feel so guilty about what happened. Poor Mr Devaux has had to leave London." Albert shook his head in dismay.

"Ah," Holmes said. "I do believe that is a blessing in disguise. We have it on good authority that Mr Devaux had dreams of retiring to Cornwall, and through this unfortunate, or should I say, fortunate, series of events, he has now achieved his dream."

"I suppose he has," Albert said, a smile appearing on his face. "Shall I let him know that everything has turned out alright, Mr Holmes? I've got his address in Cornwall from that telegram."

"No need," Holmes replied. "I will contact him. He will be given the full details of our investigation, and if he so wishes, he could return to London knowing his reputation is still intact. But I rather suspect he will stay in Cornwall."

"I think so, too," Albert replied. "I'll miss him. I might go and visit him in Cornwall. Maybe I'll move there as well. I've never seen the sea or been on a beach."

Watson said, "You must go, Albert. You'll love it."

Albert grinned. "I will go! But I'll deliver those other portraits before I dash off to the seaside." He gave his heartfelt thanks to Holmes and Watson for their help, and left the room looking much more cheerful than when he'd arrived.

"Well! What do you think about this case?" Watson asked, a bemused expression on his face.

Holmes replied, "It has been a case that ended with how it began, in a manner of speaking. I believe that by painting images of others living their dream lives, Julian Devaux has inadvertently achieved his own dream life. I will send him a brief telegram today to put his mind at rest and let him know his clients are happy with their unexpected portraits. Watson, would you be so kind as to write a detailed letter to him about our investigation? Your way with words far surpasses my own."

Watson nodded. "Of course. I shall pen the letter and explain the peculiar portrait situation to Mr Devaux."

As Watson began to write, Holmes leaned back in his chair. "It's quite remarkable, Watson, how a simple act of artistic rebellion has led to such an intriguing series of events. The power of dreams and the desire for a different life can be a potent force indeed."

Watson glanced up from his writing, a twinkle in his eye. "And to think, Holmes, all of this began with a portrait of a strange man in the Duchess of Rothbury's library!"

Holmes chuckled, his laughter echoing through the cosy confines of 221B Baker Street. "Indeed, Watson. The Duchess's portrait has certainly provided us with a most unusual case."

As Watson continued to write, Holmes allowed his mind to wander, reflecting on the curious nature of the human spirit and the lengths to which people would go to pursue their dreams. It was cases like these, he mused, that made his chosen profession all the more fascinating. He was eager for more mystifying cases to come their way.

***

Read on for the first three chapters in the next book in this series: Sherlock Holmes and The Haunted Museum

The Haunted Museum: A Sample

Chapter 1

Sherlock Holmes gazed pensively out of the window of his Baker Street lodgings, his keen, grey eyes surveying the bustling London street below. His brilliant mind, ever active and hungry for stimulation, pondered the next perplexing case that would inevitably find its way to his doorstep. Dr Watson, his stalwart companion and chronicler of their many adventures together, sat in his customary armchair by the crackling fire, the morning paper spread across his lap as he perused the day's news with a thoughtful expression.

"I say, Holmes," Watson remarked. "Listen to this peculiar headline: 'Ghostly Activities at Waxworks Museum.' Apparently, there have been numerous reports of strange and inexplicable occurrences at that museum of wax figures not far from here. You know the one; it opened about a year ago, I think."

"I know the one," Holmes replied without turning around. "Although, I haven't visited the place as yet. Perhaps I'll get around to it soon."

Watson said, "Would you like me to read this article out loud? About the strange occurrences that are happening? Some visitors claim the museum is haunted."

Holmes held up his hand. "You can stop there, Watson. I have no interest in such sensational claims. There is always a rational explanation for such so-called hauntings and supernatural activities. We have proved this many times using the power of logic and deduction."

Watson chuckled, folding the paper neatly and setting it aside on the side table. "Right, you are, Holmes. I'll read it later. No doubt the famous medium, Madam Rosalind, will make a grand appearance at the museum to commune with the alleged spirits that haunt its rooms. Doesn't she always appear at such times as these?"

At the mere mention of the medium's name, Holmes's face darkened. "She does, and with more regularity than I care for. Whenever there are claims of ghostly goings-on, Madam Rosalind is never far behind, offering her services. I would be quite content to never cross paths with that infernal woman again. Her constant attempts to offer her so-called psychic services whenever we take on a new case are most unwelcome and distracting. She has a calculating look in her eyes. One I've seen in hardened criminals. There's something untrustworthy about that woman."

With a smile, Watson said, "There will be no more talk of Madam Rosalind and her calculating eyes."

Holmes continued to gaze out of the window. His eyes narrowed as he studied the passersby. "I wonder when our next case will present itself. It feels like an eternity since we last had a mystery to unravel."

Watson replied, "It's only been a week since we concluded the affair of the missing crown. Surely you can't be growing restless already?"

"Ah, but you know me," Holmes replied. "My mind rebels at stagnation. Give me problems, give me work, give me the most puzzling mystery possible, I am in my proper atmosphere. But this inactivity is something I cannot abide."

Rising from his armchair, Watson joined his friend at the window, his eyes following Holmes's gaze to the bustling street below. "Perhaps there are new mysteries to be found right here, amongst the ordinary lives of London's citizens."

Holmes's eyes sparkled with interest. "Indeed, Watson. Take, for example, that young woman hurrying along with a bundle clutched tightly to her chest. What secrets might she be carrying?"

Watson studied the woman in question, taking note of her furtive looks and how she seemed to shrink away from the other pedestrians. "Perhaps she's fleeing from an unhappy marriage, or maybe she's stolen something valuable and fears being caught."

"Very possible," Holmes said, his attention already shifting to another figure on the street. "And what about that elderly gentleman, walking with a pronounced limp and a faraway look in his eyes?"

"A war veteran, I'd wager," Watson replied, his own military background allowing him to recognise the tell tale signs. "Haunted by the memories of battles long past, and perhaps nursing a wound that never fully healed."

Holmes nodded, a hint of admiration in his voice. "Your medical expertise serves you well, my dear friend."

As they continued to observe the passersby, Holmes's keen eyes alighted upon a young man who seemed to be in a great hurry, his face pale and his hands trembling. "Now, Watson, what do you make of that fellow?"

Watson furrowed his brow, studying the man intently. "He appears to be in a state of great agitation, Holmes. Perhaps he's just received some terrible news, or maybe he's fleeing from some sort of trouble."

"Ah, but look closer, Watson," Holmes urged. "Notice the ink stains on his fingers, the slight bulge in his coat pocket that suggests a small notebook, and the way he glances left and right, as if searching for someone or something."

"A journalist, then?" Watson ventured, beginning to see the clues that Holmes had so easily discerned.

"Precisely, Watson. And not just any journalist, but one who has stumbled upon a story of great importance. The question is, what could have made him so unsettled?"

His tone deliberately solemn, Watson suggested, "Is it possible there's been a development in that perplexing haunting at the museum? Maybe our dear acquaintance, Madam Rosalind, is due to pay a visit there at any moment and despatch any impish phantoms. And our young journalist out there doesn't want to miss a second of this latest development."

Sherlock let out a loud laugh that startled Watson. "You could very well be correct! I've half a mind to run after that fellow and see where he is going."

"Even if it leads to Madam Rosalind?" Watson jested.

"Ah, you have a point. We'll leave the fellow alone." He looked left and right. "Now, who else do we spy out there?"

As they continued to observe the street below, a particular figure caught Sherlock's eye. A man, dressed in a fashionable hat and an expensive-looking overcoat, was pacing back and forth in front of their building, his movements erratic and hesitant.

"Watson," Holmes said, "do you see that man down there? The one in the hat and overcoat?"

Watson leaned closer to the window, squinting to get a better look. "Yes, I see him. He seems rather agitated, doesn't he?"

"He does," Holmes agreed, his attention never leaving the man. "His behaviour is most peculiar. It's as if he's wrestling with some internal dilemma, unsure of whether to approach our door or not."

They watched as the man took a few determined steps towards the entrance of 221B Baker Street, only to abruptly turn away at the last moment. He walked a short distance, then paused, his shoulders slumping as if in defeat.

"He's changed his mind," Watson observed. "But why? What could be troubling him so?"

Holmes replied, "I suspect we may have a potential client on our hands. A man who is grappling with a problem so perplexing, so overwhelming, that he fears to even seek our assistance. Notice the way he keeps glancing at our windows, the tension in his shoulders. There is something troubling him. Something he needs to share with another person."

As if on cue, the man turned around once more, his steps now filled with a newfound determination as he approached the door of 221B Baker Street. Holmes and Watson watched as he raised his hand, hesitating for the briefest of moments before finally knocking.

The sound echoed through the house, a sharp and insistent rap that seemed to hang in the air. Moments later, the door was opened and Mrs Hudson's muffled voice could be heard as she greeted the visitor.

"Well, Watson," Holmes said, a glint of excitement in his eyes, "it appears our lull in activity is about to come to an end. Shall we see what mystery this gentleman brings to our doorstep?"

Holmes dashed to his chair, urging Watson to do the same, insisting they must be seated before their guest's arrival, lest he suspect they had been peering at him through the window.

Watson looked as if he might say that they had been doing exactly that, but thought better of it and instead hurried to his own chair, swiftly arranging himself in a posture of studied indifference.

They waited as Mrs Hudson's footsteps grew louder, accompanied by the heavier tread of their mysterious visitor. The door to their sitting room opened.

Chapter 2

Mrs Hudson entered the sitting room, followed closely by the visitor. "Gentlemen," she said, "this is Mr Alfred Chamberlain. He's here to see you about a matter of some urgency."

The man took off his hat and overcoat and gave them to Mrs Hudson, who already had her hands extended towards him.

Sherlock rose from his chair, extending his hand in greeting. "Mr Chamberlain, welcome. I am Sherlock

Holmes, and this is my colleague, Dr John Watson. Please, come in and have a seat."

Mr Chamberlain was a portly man in his late fifties. He had bushy eyebrows and a jovial face, and was dressed in a tailored suit that strained slightly at the buttons. His handshake was firm. "Pleased to meet you, both of you."

Mrs Hudson turned to Sherlock. "Shall I bring up some refreshments, Mr Holmes?"

"Yes, thank you, Mrs Hudson. That would be most appreciated," Sherlock replied with a nod.

Mrs Hudson left the room, closing the door behind her. Chamberlain was invited to take a seat. A light sheen of perspiration lay upon his brow.

"Now, Mr Chamberlain," Sherlock began, settling back into his own chair, "what brings you to our doorstep today? I can see that you are troubled by something."

Chamberlain cleared his throat, his glance darting between Sherlock and Watson. "Well, Mr Holmes, it's a bit of a delicate matter. I'm not quite sure how to begin."

Sherlock said, "Mr Chamberlain, I assure you that no problem is ever too delicate for our assistance. Please, feel free to speak freely."

Chamberlain nodded, taking a deep breath. "You see, gentlemen, I am the proprietor of a waxworks museum. It opened over a year ago, and we've been doing quite well. That is, until recently."

Watson, who had been listening intently, suddenly sat up straighter. "I say, Mr Chamberlain, your museum wouldn't happen to be the one mentioned in this morning's paper, would it? The one with the alleged ghostly activity?"

He held up the newspaper, the headline clearly visible. Chamberlain's face reddened, and he shifted uncomfortably in his seat.

"Yes, Dr Watson, I'm afraid that is indeed my establishment. I don't know how the press got news of it. But I must stress that I do not believe in the supernatural whatsoever. There must be a logical explanation for the strange occurrences."

Sherlock's eyes lit up with interest. "Ah, I am glad to hear that your views on the supernatural match my own. I'm eager to learn more of these strange occurrences you speak of. Please, Mr Chamberlain, do go on."

Chamberlain settled back in his chair. "It started recently. Small things at first. Objects moving on their own, strange noises suddenly filling the air, ghostly figures moving through the corridors. But then it escalated."

"I see," Sherlock said. "Please, continue."

Chamberlain paused, as if steeling himself for what he was about to say next. "One of our most popular exhibits, a wax figure of William Shakespeare, had disappeared, leaving only his quill behind. He turned up later, standing next to Captain Blackbeard. The two figures had been turned towards each other as if in cahoots. You should have heard the complaints we received about that, especially from a local historian who had decided to visit us that day. And then, just two days later, a figure of Jack the Ripper vanished entirely from its usual position, only to reappear in a different part of the museum which was created for our younger visitors. Some of the smallest children erupted into tears when they saw the menacing look on Jack's face. Oh! The complaints I received from furious parents that day!"

Watson's eyes widened. "Good heavens!"

Sherlock, however, remained impassive. "Forgive me for asking, Mr Chamberlain, but are these merely pranks or publicity stunts? I'm not saying they were committed by you, but maybe someone you employ?"

Chamberlain shook his head vehemently. "The people I employ would never stoop to such a thing. I trust them implicitly, no doubt about that. What troubles me, is how the newspapers have labelled this as ghostly activity. That isn't good for my business and visitor numbers are already falling. I know there must be a reasonable explanation behind these strange events, but I'm at a loss to think what that could be."

At that moment, Mrs Hudson returned with a tray of tea and biscuits. She set it down on the table, casting a curious glance at Chamberlain before leaving the room once more.

As Sherlock poured the tea, he said, "Mr Chamberlain, I am pleased to hear that you seek a logical explanation for the strange occurrences at your museum. From the details I have so far, I suspect a human hand is behind these, and not that of a spectral nature."

He handed a cup to Chamberlain, who accepted it with a grateful nod. "Thank you, Mr Holmes. I knew coming to you was the right decision, even though it took some courage to knock on your door, considering the nature of my problem. I was so embarrassed at the prospect of asking you to look into my supposed haunted museum. Will you help me get to the bottom of this mystery?"

Sherlock smiled. "My dear Mr Chamberlain, nothing would give me greater pleasure. Dr Watson and I will be happy to lend our assistance."

Watson, who had been helping himself to a biscuit, looked up in surprise. "We will?"

Sherlock shot him a smile. "Of course we will, Watson. A case like this, where we get to debunk supernatural rumours, is just the sort of challenge I relish." He turned back to Chamberlain. "Now, Mr Chamberlain, please tell us everything you know about these activities. Leave out no detail, no matter how insignificant it may seem."

Chamberlain, looking visibly relieved, began to recount his tale in earnest. "It all started about three weeks ago," he said. "A young lady, quite distressed, came rushing to me, claiming that one of the waxworks in an exhibit room had moved."

Holmes said, "Moved, you say? In what manner?"

"She said it had shifted slightly to the left, right before her eyes. The poor girl was convinced it had come to life. She let out a scream that echoed through the entire museum. She ran out of the exhibit room in a state of sheer terror. It was that scream that made me run towards her. She looked as if she was about to faint."

Watson's eyebrows rose in surprise. "That must have been quite a shock for her."

Chamberlain nodded, his expression grim. "At the time, I tried to reassure her, suggesting that perhaps a sudden, strong gust of wind had caused the movement. After all, these things do happen in old buildings like ours."

Holmes, however, seemed unconvinced. "A gust of wind? Was the waxwork figure in an enclosed exhibit room or near a doorway?"

Chamberlain shifted uncomfortably in his seat. "It was in an enclosed room, and, well, it was the only explanation I could think of at the moment. I didn't want to alarm the young lady further."

"Understandable," Holmes said, his tone neutral. "Please, do go on."

"I thought nothing more of it," Chamberlain continued, "until I started receiving other complaints. More visitors claimed to have seen the waxworks moving, and then there were the sounds..."

"Sounds?" Watson asked.

"Yes, Dr Watson. Eerie noises, coming from all directions. Whispers, creaks, and even the occasional moan. It was as if the museum itself had come alive."

Holmes asked, "And when did these sounds begin?"

"A few days after the first incident with the young lady," Chamberlain replied. "It wasn't long before rumours started circulating that the museum was haunted. Visitor numbers began to fall, and then the newspaper got wind of the story and those rumours have increased tenfold."

"I can well imagine," Sherlock said in understanding.

Chamberlain continued, "Mr Holmes, if these rumours persist, I fear my museum will be forced to close its doors. I simply cannot afford to lose any more business."

Holmes nodded, his expression one of deep thought. "I understand your concerns, Mr Chamberlain. Now, do you have any suspects in mind? Someone who would like to see the closing of your museum?"

Chamberlain looked up, his eyes wide. "Yes, Mr Holmes. There is someone who I believe would like to see my museum fail and take great joy in it."

"And who might that be?" Holmes asked.

Chamberlain said, "Marcus Bramwell. He's my ex-business partner. I'm almost certain he's the one behind this."

"What makes you suspect him?" Holmes asked.

Chamberlain sighed. "We had a falling out three years ago over a financial matter. I'd rather not go into the details, but suffice it to say, it was a messy affair. Bramwell has been out for revenge ever since."

Watson frowned. "Revenge is a powerful motive. Has he made any direct threats?"

"Not directly, no," Chamberlain admitted. "But I wouldn't put it past him to employ people to sabotage the museum on his behalf. He's a cunning man, and he knows how to cover his tracks."

Holmes nodded. "Interesting. And where might we find this Marcus Bramwell?"

Chamberlain said, "He's set up a rival tourist attraction, Bramwell's Hall of Scientific Marvels. It's probably receiving all the tourists who no longer visit the waxworks museum."

Holmes said, "Bramwell's Hall of Scientific Marvels? I've heard of it. It's been gaining quite a reputation of late."

"Yes, it has," Chamberlain said, his tone bitter. "While my museum struggles, his thrives. It's as if he's stealing my customers right from under my nose."

Watson looked at Holmes. "What do you think, Holmes? Could Bramwell be behind these disturbances?"

Holmes tapped his chin, deep in thought. "It's certainly a possibility, Watson. A man with a grudge and a rival business. It's a classic motive. Mr Chamberlain, Dr Watson and I will pay a visit to your ex-business partner and see what he has to say for himself. After that, I would like to visit your museum, to examine the scene of these disturbances firsthand."

Chamberlain nodded eagerly. "Of course, Mr Holmes. I'll give you a personal tour. When would be convenient for you?"

Holmes glanced at the clock on the mantelpiece. "Shall we say, three o'clock this afternoon? That should give us ample time to speak with Mr Bramwell and then make our way to your establishment."

"Three o'clock it is," Chamberlain agreed, rising from his seat. "Thank you, Mr Holmes, Dr Watson. I can't tell you how much I appreciate your help."

Holmes also stood, shaking Chamberlain's hand. "We'll do our best to get to the bottom of this mystery, Mr Chamberlain. You have my word."

With that, Chamberlain took his leave, the relief on his face palpable. As the door closed behind him, Watson turned to Holmes.

"Well, Holmes, what do you make of it all?" he asked.

Holmes picked up his pipe, turning it over in his hands. "It's a curious case, Watson. There is much to unravel here, one of them the intriguing matter of the financial dispute between the two businessmen. I would like to find out what happened there. It could be related to what's occurring at the museum now. Let's speak with Marcus Bramwell and see what he has to say."

Watson nodded, reaching for his hat and coat. "Then let's be off, Holmes. The game, as they say, is afoot."

Holmes laughed. "Indeed, it is, Watson. Indeed, it is."

Chapter 3

Holmes and Watson hailed a hansom cab and made their way to Bramwell's Hall of Scientific Marvels. As they approached the building, they couldn't help but be impressed by its modern design. The clean lines and large, plate-glass windows stood in stark contrast to the gothic architecture of the surrounding buildings. Electric lights framed the entrance, beckoning visitors to come and witness the marvels of technology within.

After paying for their tickets, they entered the impressive building and found themselves in a sleek and utilitarian interior, designed to showcase the exhibits rather than the architecture itself. The main hall was filled with interactive displays and machines, each demonstrating the latest technological advancements of the era. A working model of a steam engine caught Watson's eye, while Holmes was drawn to the early electrical devices on display.

It was clear that Bramwell's attraction appealed to the public's fascination with science and innovation, offering a glimpse into the future that was both exciting and awe-inspiring.

As they were examining a particularly intricate display, a tall and distinguished figure approached them. With his neatly trimmed beard and penetrating blue eyes, the man exuded confidence and intelligence. His salt and pepper hair lent him an air of distinguished maturity, while his impeccably tailored dark suit spoke of his success and status.

"Ah, Mr Sherlock Holmes and Dr John Watson, I presume?" the man said, his voice smooth and charming. "I am Marcus Bramwell. I saw you through the window of my office and recognised you immediately from photographs that have appeared in the newspapers. May I ask, is your visit one of pleasure or of business?"

Holmes said, "Our visit is of a business nature, Mr Bramwell. We were hoping to have a word with you regarding a matter of some importance."

Bramwell smiled, but there was a coldness behind it. "Of course, gentlemen. Please, follow me to my office, where we can speak more privately."

As they followed Bramwell to his office, Holmes noticed the approving looks the man received from several women they passed. It was clear that Bramwell's charm and enigmatic nature made him a favourite among the fairer sex.

Once they were seated in Bramwell's office, the man leaned back in his chair. "So, gentlemen, what brings you to my humble establishment?"

Holmes explained, "We're here on behalf of Mr Alfred Chamberlain, the owner of the waxwork museum across town."

Bramwell's smile tightened almost imperceptibly. "Ah, yes. Poor Alfred. I heard he's been having some trouble lately."

Holmes continued, "He believes that someone may be deliberately sabotaging his business. As a result, his visitor numbers have dwindled."

Bramwell raised an eyebrow. "And he thinks the person responsible for the sabotage is me?"

Holmes didn't answer immediately, instead studying Bramwell's reaction. After a moment, he said, "He mentioned that you two had a falling out some years ago."

Bramwell waved a hand dismissively. "A minor disagreement, nothing more. Certainly nothing that would drive me to sabotage his business."

Watson spoke, his tone curious. "Mr Bramwell, is it possible that your establishment has benefited from the misfortunes of Mr Chamberlain's museum?"

Bramwell's eyes flashed, but his voice remained calm. "Dr Watson, success in business is often a matter of seizing opportunities when they arise. If Alfred's misfortune has driven more customers to my doors, well, that's simply the nature of competition. Was there anything else? I've got a busy day ahead of me."

Holmes said, "Mr Bramwell, would you like to know the specific acts of sabotage that have taken place at Mr Chamberlain's establishment? Aren't you the least bit curious?"

Bramwell retrieved a folded newspaper from the side of his desk, a knowing smile on his face. "I'm already aware of what's happened, at least according to the press." He tapped the newspaper with his finger.

"And what do you make of the gossip that the troubles are of a supernatural nature?" Holmes asked.

Bramwell scoffed, his eyes narrowing. "Not likely. I don't believe in any of that nonsense."

Watson asked, "Do you have any theories about what might be behind these incidents, Mr Bramwell?"

Bramwell answered, "It could be an insider job."

Holmes raised an eyebrow. "Mr Chamberlain assured us that his staff are loyal."

A cold smile spread across Bramwell's face. "That isn't the case with some of them. I suggest you talk to the staff more closely, especially one of the sculptors who has been overheard in a public house complaining about how he's been treated by Mr Chamberlain."

"And do you have a name for this disgruntled sculptor?" Holmes asked.

Bramwell shrugged. "I've no idea. Isn't it your job to find that out, Mr Holmes? You are a detective, after all."

Holmes stood, buttoning his jacket, not appreciating the mockery in Bramwell's voice. "Thank you for your time and the information you've provided. It has been most enlightening."

Watson stood as well, nodding to Bramwell. "Yes, thank you, Mr Bramwell."

As they left Bramwell's office and walked away, Holmes turned to Watson, his brow furrowed in thought. "I believe there's more to this than meets the eye. Bramwell's demeanour and his readiness to point the finger at Chamberlain's staff raises some interesting questions."

Watson nodded. "You think he might have ulterior motives?"

"It's a possibility we can't ignore," Holmes said, his pace quickening as they exited the Hall of Scientific Marvels. "We need to speak with Chamberlain's staff, particularly this sculptor Bramwell mentioned. But we must also keep an open mind. There could be other factors at play here."

They hailed a cab and asked the driver to take them to Mr Chamberlain's Waxwork Museum. As they settled in their seats, Holmes' mind was already filling with questions and theories. He was determined to solve the mystery as soon as possible.

****

A note from the author

For as long as I can remember, I have loved reading mystery books. It started with Enid Blyton's Famous Five, and The Secret Seven. As I got older, I progressed to Agatha Christie books, and of course, Sir Arthur Conan Doyle's Sherlock Holmes.

I love the characters of Sherlock Holmes and Dr Watson, and the Victorian era that the stories are set in. It seemed only natural that one day, I would write some of my own Sherlock stories. I love creating new mysteries for Mr Holmes, and his trusty companion, Dr John Watson. It's not just the era itself that seems to ignite ideas within me; it's also the characters who were around at that time, and the lives they led.

This story has been checked for errors, but if you see anything we have missed and you'd like to let us know about them, please email mabel@mabelswift.com

You can hear about my new releases by signing up to my newsletter www.mabelswift.com As a thank you for subscribing, I will send you a free short story: Sherlock Holmes and The Curious Clock.

If you'd like to contact me, you can get in touch via mabel@mabelswift.com I'd be delighted to hear from you.

Best wishes

Mabel

Printed in Great Britain
by Amazon